Good Citizen Sarah

Virginia Kroll

Illustrated by **Nancy Cote**

Albert Whitman & Company, Morton Grove, Illinois

To Sara DeAnthony, Sara Knapp, Sarah Machajewski,
and Sarah Paulick, who are all good citizens.—V.K.

To Collin, the newest member of the family, 3/18/07.
All my love.—N.C.

The Way I Act Books:

Cristina Keeps a Promise • *Forgiving a Friend* • *Good Citizen Sarah* • *Good Neighbor Nicholas*
Honest Ashley • *Jason Takes Responsibility* • *Makayla Cares about Others* • *Ryan Respects*

The Way I Feel Books:

When I Care about Others • *When I Feel Angry* • *When I Feel Good about Myself* • *When I Feel Jealous*
When I Feel Sad • *When I Feel Scared* • *When I Miss You*

Library of Congress Cataloging-in-Publication Data

Kroll, Virginia L.
Good citizen Sarah / by Virginia Kroll ; illustrated by Nancy Cote.
p. cm.—(The way I act ; #8)
Summary: On an unexpected snow day, Sarah learns that being a good citizen is not just about obeying laws—
citizenship also involves being a good neighbor and helping others when they need it.
ISBN 10: 0-8075-2992-3 (hardcover)   ISBN 13: 978-0-8075-2992-8 (hardcover)
[1. Citizenship—Fiction. 2. Conduct of life—Fiction. 3. Neighbors—Fiction.
4. Snow—Fiction.] I. Cote, Nancy, ill. II. Title.
PZ7.K9227Gk 2007 [E]—dc22 2007001340

Design by Carol Gildar.

For information about Albert Whitman & Company,
please visit our web site at www.albertwhitman.com.

Just before Sarah went to bed, Mom said, "Sarah, I almost forgot. A surprise came for you in today's mail."

Sarah quickly opened her package. "Wow, it's the computer game I wanted from Grandma! Can Mary and Noah come over to play it after school tomorrow?"

"Yes, they can." Mom smiled.

Sarah gave her toy pig, Oink, a happy hug.

The next morning, Mom announced, "No school today. A big snowstorm blew in overnight."

Sarah couldn't believe her eyes. Snow covered everything except the broken branches that littered the ground. She swung Oink into the air in celebration. "Yippee! I can play my new video game all day!"

"Not until the power comes back on," her mother said.

Dad came into the kitchen, stomping his boots. "Looks like nobody is going anywhere today," he reported. "Snow and fallen branches are blocking everything. I'll get busy clearing our yard and driveway, and then we can help our neighbors."

Sarah bundled up and went outside. Throughout the neighborhood, saws and snowblowers buzzed and shovels scraped. Just as Sarah reached for a shovel, Noah called, "Hey, Sarah, come build a snowman with me and Mary."

"Okay," Sarah said. But there was no room to roll snowballs. Even walking was hard with all the branches in the way.

Sarah and her friends decided to go inside and play board games. "What's for lunch?" Sarah asked her mother. "I'm hungry."

"Eat yogurt and cereal for now, Sarah. We're out of bread and cold cuts. These sandwiches are for Dad and the neighbors who are working."

Noah and Mary decided to go home. "We'll come back when the power's on," Noah said.

Sarah pouted. No video game, no TV, no lunch—and now, no friends. She went to the family room and plopped into the computer chair. "I wish I had a magic wand so I could turn the power on," she said.

Dad came back in to pick up lunch for the neighbors.

"Whew!" he panted. "It's a mess out there. But we're cleaning up, bit by bit. Lucky thing our neighborhood is filled with so many good citizens."

Sarah frowned crinkles into her forehead. *Good citizens?* she wondered. Her class had talked about being good citizens and not breaking any laws. What did cutting trees and shoveling snow have to do with that?

Sarah glanced over at Mrs. Warren's house. She could see her friend sitting at her kitchen table. Sarah thought Mrs. Warren looked sad. Usually they shared a wave and a smile across the way.

Just then, a lamp blinked on. "Yay! The power's fixed. Now I can play!" Sarah shouted, running to turn on the computer.

While it was loading, Sarah looked out the window again. Mrs. Warren waved, but she wasn't smiling. Sarah wondered if she was warm enough. Did she have something to eat? Who would shovel her driveway and clear her yard?

The video game came on. It was so cool! But then Sarah thought of Mrs. Warren, and Dad's words popped back into her mind.

Sarah made a decision. She could play her new game later. More important things needed to be done right now.

Sarah bundled up again. "Mom, I'm going to check on Mrs. Warren, okay?"

"What a good idea!" Mom said.

Sarah went outside. The neighbors were working hard. The O'Neill and McFall kids were shoveling while their parents cut tree limbs. Even little Courtney Kenworthy was stacking neat piles of twigs. They were like one big team, each doing a little part. Maybe being a good citizen isn't just about obeying laws, Sarah thought. It's about being a good neighbor and helping others when they need it. That's why Dad called them all good citizens.

Mrs. Warren was happy to see Sarah. "Why, you're an angel," she said. "Could you please open Pearl's cat food? My hands are stiff from the cold."

The white cat meowed and rubbed against Sarah's legs, happy to see her, too.

After feeding Pearl,
Sarah asked Mrs. Warren
what else she could do.

"Well, I can't seem to find my reading glasses."
Sarah searched and found them on the hall table.

She noticed Mrs. Warren's bag of garbage by the door
and took it out to the trash can.

As Sarah was leaving, Mary and Noah were coming over.

"Power's on, Sarah. We can play your computer game now. Let's go!" said Mary.

Sarah wanted to play her new game, but she knew this wasn't the right time. "How about we be good citizens instead? We could help clean up the neighborhood. If we each do a little work, it can add up to a lot."

"Sarah's right," said Mary. "And it will be fun to help."

Noah sighed. "Okay," he said. "We can play the game tomorrow."

They began by picking up piles of twigs
and hauling branches to the curb.

They shoveled a path on their side of the street
for Mr. Yormick, the mailman.

They cleared the fire hydrant in front of Mrs. Warren's house, then shoveled her driveway, too.

"Wow! You were right, Sarah. We really did a lot!" Noah said.

All day long the neighborhood was filled with people sawing and shoveling.

Sarah went to the Bartelos' house after dinner. She stayed inside with Drew and Zach while their parents worked outside. They sang songs, read stories, and played puppets. Sarah taught them how to count from one to ten in Spanish.

As Sarah got ready for bed, she yawned. She was *so* tired. But it was a good feeling of tiredness.

"I'm proud of you, Sarah," said Dad as he kissed her good night.

Mom tucked her in and said, "Sleep tight, good citizen Sarah."

Sarah liked the sound of that.

She cuddled her pig. But before she could whisper, "Good night, Oink," she was already fast asleep.